Ode To Life

Tahashin Shaira

Dedication

I would probably never know that I can write a poetry book unless I wrote the first poem of this book. Why not dedicating the book to its 1st poem "Asian Dream"?

CONTENTS

ACKNOWLEDGMENTS

Life has the potential to come up with anything and many things you never thought of. I am grateful to life; this book would never be complete unless life had cut me, choked me, and blessed me with all its blessings. I am thankful to myself for believing that I have the least potential not to waste this life.

I am grateful to my mother for offering her support when I needed it the most. I am grateful to my friends and my sister for believing in me. I am grateful to my brother who helped me design the book cover and always lit me up with his jokes.

Last but not the least, I am grateful to all of you for giving my endeavor a read.

Thank you.

Tahashin

Asian Dream

I was never born as a human child
With blood, flesh, and organs,
I was born as a girl.

I was not a social demand;
Of course-
What good is a girl of?
I was not a familial pride
As you might guess-
Having me was a pain my parents couldn't confess.
My aunt, who too is a woman,
Showered sympathy, instead of love.
Soon the sympathy changed to sorrow,
Sorrow as they came to know:
It wasn't a daughter with pearls in her eyes;
Or a piece of flesh- the color similar to ice.

It was a midget daughter-
A black daughter-
An ugly daughter-
An unhealthy daughter -
It was a DAUGHTER!
A DAUGHTER, a DAUGHTER, a DAUGHTER
A daughter who only cried,
A daughter who only cried.

There wasn't a thing else to search in me,
Neither did they let me be what I was meant to be.
All they did -
was to handle some rules to be maintained,
As I was always taken to be granted.
I had no choice to choose my life,
How dare a girl do what they like?
For every assaults they rendered us-
I had never a chance to debate on,
How come a girl goes against the social norms?

I was a girl with a solved destiny
That many other girls had if you search the history.
Whether I dream to fly till the sun
It's always home that I cannot run.
With my hands, legs, heart, and mind
Having tied to follow the society blind.
I forgot to search the me in me
I forgot what I once dreamt to be.
And off following what they told me to,
I realized there's always discomfort in the shoe.
"You are a girl; adapt to it!"
Came the voice when I tried to dismiss.
I wasn't surprised by this absurd threat.
For that's how a girl- life was led.

I adapted-
To injustice.
To the vicious fist.
To the partiality
of the society;
To the versatility
of solitary.

And I was declared the epitome of sacrifice-
In the epic or the fables authors write.
The was the caress to the billow
Of the fire any girl- willow.
And one day as I woke up from the poems-
Left Byron and Keats-
Made it to my streets-
I watched the open sky, flying birds,
The rushes of lives heaving me to crux.

I had felt so grounded.
I realized it soon-
Had the society, true:
But I myself, too
Had taken me to be granted.

I put an end to my dread
Not with words, axe, or hate.
I did it through silence.
I started working on my own-
Dawn till dusk, skin to bone.

I was mesmerized by the power I had earned
Not as a human child, but as a girl.
I started understanding: my voice is different.
Without speaking, it speaks for the unspoken.

And thus I started moving on,
A new girl inside me was born.
I could sense the world behind me-
Being happy or jealous as they could be.
I too could see my girls rising up,
Making their way through patriarchy's trap.

And as time passes, it passes the past,
And I look back, look back and smirk.
I feel proud to have born as a girl;
Instead of being your "social charm"

My Mother Hadn't Seen The Sky

My mother used to be a household material.
She was no different from the table-chair.
She was more of a kitchen sink,
Holding the filth of the house stiff.
The sink was always used,
But nobody cared if rust interfered.
And when the sink wouldn't work properly,
There would be piles of dishes gathered around.
A dramatic plea of the house-
A dramatic plea of the house she had been.

My mother had never seen the sky;
She had a limit till her balcony.
She'd often hold the grills of her window,
Losing sight to the blueless of the sky.
Less of a sky had it been,
For she never knew the immensity of it.

I often gaze at the sky as I gaze at her.
Saddening she never knew the beauties of the stars,
She hadn't ever seen free flies under cloud,
She doesn't know the colors of roses when sunray follows.
She had barely known the dark of thunder,
For she passed her whole life in her only shelter.
For she had never seen the glory of the sky,
She had never understood the depth of the life:
Rather replaced it with the word "sacrifice".

Sometimes, I look at the depth of her eyes.
I cry she needs to see the sky.

I could never tell her the link of life to the sky,
For my philosophy and her practical view never had a tie.

But then as I noticed the existence of the sink,
Late but I looked at the household utensils.
I could realize:
No glance to the sky, does she need to give a try-
For she herself had been the sky.

Meaning Of Life

How many sleepless night have you passed-
Trying to convince thyself to work hard.
How many time did you tell yourself
For not to hold onto useless stuff.

I suppose you still stay wide awake,
Trying to figure out the lessons, life's take.
I believe you still wait for a cue,
To direct you to what to do.

But I hope with time you'll know,
Life's not all about hard work.
It's not always the effort that's worth.

Life's much more about-
Sitting on a balcony chair with a coffee mug,
Walking down the road with an empty heart.
Life's too about being in pace, not in peace.
Life means to survive through this race.

I hope one day you will learn,
Life is a beautiful poem in turn.

This Life

If this life had any value, I would never sabotage my love;
for love would have its value too.
I would have adored love,
Through the melodies of its hustling scars-
Embellishing its entity with painful color,
But I would never let it go.

If this life had any value, I would rather flee from the prison
I live; for freedom would have its value too.
I would walk barefoot over the grass,
Trample the limp of the earth,
I perhaps would die through the vigil of grace,
But I would never forsake my freedom.

If this life had any value, I would forever foster my devotion,
for my devotion would have its value too.
I would have polished every of my wishes,
Would have sailed my raft till bruises.
Would forever hold myself tight,
But never let my desires die.

But I know under all the circumstances, this life that I am
living has no value.
It has no aim set,
It has an end foreseen,
It has no turn of luck,
It has somewhere got stuck.

That I know under all the circumstances, this life that I am living has no value.
It tries in vain,
Even in spring it rains,
It stirs sadness with existence,
It contracts the span of happiness.

And for its enormous poverty,
I try every moment to get a new entity.
I try to trade this life-
For a mere chance to thrive.
I try to trade this in lieu of a piece of smile;
A plateful of peace,
A handful of grace.

And I know I will someday change this life; for change is constant.
No good to bad,
No blatant surrender.
Each step forward,
Nothing holding back.

And I know I will someday improve this life; for improvement is a paramount.
I will chase the sun till the moon,
Wander valleys, mountains I would stroll.
I will tear apart the old traits of me.
And grow lotus where muds have been.

And I know someday I will overpass my fears; for fears only oppress me.
I will grow like the banyan tree-
With its greatness sheltering the heaven.
At the zenith there will be me,
Underneath my agonies trodden.

And I know someday I will be happy; for happiness will be my feat.
My happiness will be my winter,
My spring and my autumn.
For it might rain sometimes,
Still happiness would survive.

And someday when I die,
After outliving this life-
I will know there's no better fit
Than the life that I have lived.

Sullen Air

Air streamed through my window,
And I chased to cease the flow.

I glassed the window, turned my curtain-
I no longer would feel the wind was certain.

I thus barriered what was bothering me
And realized that's how life's supposed to be.

For I can never entirely release a load,
But I can always hinder its flow.

Writing My Life down

With my pens stuck on my notebook,
I have no words to express my heart.
I know the struggle survival took,
I suffocate where my story would start.

I keep the pen stationary on my page.
The color of the pen reminds me of my rage.
I look at the emptiness of the surface,
I feel it's my life this page reciprocate.

And down the memory lane as I look back,
I find butterflies and birds singing my hymn.

I suddenly realize life will never be the same,
And life will constantly change.

Death Has Visited Me Twice

Death had visited me twice till then.
First time when I was ready,
I myself called for him.
I appealed that he shows me his way-
So that I could escape my fate.
Death, that time, didn't take me with him.
But he came closer,
He breathed over my lungs.
I could smell the taste of it.
I pleaded and pleaded; he didn't listen to me.

Death that time went away with his empty hand.
Death that time meant he cannot be owned.

The next time death came to me,
I was too occupied living my life.
I forgot that death might come.
I was too busy hatching butterflies
To notice that death was here.

And such as he came again,
I pleaded: please go away.
And I was frozen inside-out
What I, long ago had asked for, ain't a lie.
For death was no lie, was no lie.
Death- a destination, death no sprite.

Irony Of Blessing

I was elated to find spring in winter,
Just as I was happy when it rained in autumn.
I always adorned the untimely blessings-

But then I realized things were wrong-
When I found people concerned.

What blessings do blesses offer,
When they pick the wrong time to come?

Realize

Sitting on a park bench-
Along with thousands of unknown birds,
For the first time in this life
Could I realize:
It was never loneliness that I was afraid of-
All along it has been the fear of being alone.

And as I keep myself steady on the bench,
I watch people coming and leaving with full sense.
For the first time in this life
Could I realize:
I was never afraid of people leaving my side,
I was only tired of the blank spaces they would place in my life.

And as I pick myself to walk my path,
Step after step I trod the road I craft-
For the first time in this life
Could I realize:
I can walk alone the scars people leave,
I can make my existence alone a fair trip.

Crowd Of Me

In this crowd of people,
Are the vast versions of me.
Some are what I used to be,
Few what I wish to be.
Some who want to be like me,
And me who don't know who she is.

In this crowd that I surround myself in,
There's that past version of me,
Who's careless of who she is.
There's that now version of me,
Who wants to figure out what her existence means.
Then there's my cherished version too,
Reaching destination that I'm yet to figure out.

Existence

I haven't seen butterflies these days-
I haven't seen no water, no rain.
There haven't been any soft wind touching me lately,
I don't remember the last time snow drained.

For I've been too busy with myself-
To care about anything else.
And, too often, now I feel so void,
Engraving question to my existence.

3 AM

3 AM in the morning,
Behind the closed window is a bird chirping
Slowly and softly, it's taking its time.
Outside my closed door,
left to the kitchen is sleeping my mom.
3 AM is just a night for her, 3 AM is no fantasy she thinks of.
Outside my house was a dog barking, when I passed the gate at 7 o'clock.
Barks never reach me around, who knows if It still has the sound.
If 3 AM has any value to the dog-

3 AM in the morning, I open my window.
The chirping of that unknown bird
Riving the rib of darkness,
I call the darkness my emptiness.
I call my emptiness my shadow.
My shadow dissolves me–
I don't find the bird any nearer,
I don't know to which tree it might belong.
3 AM ain't no time to search for a bird.

3 AM in the morning, I open my door.
Left to the kitchen is my mother's room.
3 AM is when I unlock her half-locked door.
The sound of sleep, the smell of it gets me cold.
3 AM has nothing to do with this woman.
Maybe she's passed enough 3AMs not to care further,
Or she's never faced a 3 AM phase at a 3 AM so far.
I can't really tell- looking at her calmness;

But I wonder,
Each 3 AM in the morning, I wonder,

What is this 3 AM famous for?
Solitary or the coldness of the hearts,
Why is it 3 AM so far?
Why there's no room for the heart to bleed,
To the people whom we choose to be with.
Why there's comfort in expressing the tears
To the midnights' solitary, rather to the humans.
I never get out of the puzzle 3 AM puts me in,
I only breathe through the suffocation of it

3 AM in the morning,
I come back to my room
I look at the clock, I look into the mirror
My mirror reflects the clock,
The clock reflects me.
3 AM is when I determine, there's so much more to heave.
3 AM is when sadness leaves it gloom,
3AM is when hopes hop into the room.
3 AM, I suppose, is a blessing prodigy,
Probably that's the 3 AM's beauty of melancholy.

Do Not Grief

Do not grief when I will leave,
Never anticipate that I might knit.
I was never born to stay,
Never was meant to be defined innate.

I have my destiny in an unknown path,
I will walk along the road till I reach the end.

I might pause a while when you wail,
Yet, as destined, I would continue my steps.
But never anticipate that I might knit.
And do not grief when I will leave.

Dear Death

Dear Death,
I put a "dear" before I call by your name,
I often use curse words too.
But I mostly leave you unaddressed.

Last time I called you was a rainy day without a single drop of rain.
I offered you my life that resembled the day;
And you denied offering an ear to me.

The one before the last time,
I called you as warm as I could.
I embraced my pains inside my stomach,
And I asked if you could tear me apart.
You laughingly said to me-
"Heart must be fulfilled with grief,
Call me when it overflows, for I know it never will."

It never did,
But I recalled you one time again.
This time, I was as warm as cold,
And I put a "dear" before I utter your name.
I call to tell you this time, never do grieves inundate:
They are birds inside a cage.
Who flitter the wings to death,
But fly away when escaped.

Art Of Proceeding

Thousands of footprints I've left behind,
Few more steps I have got to go.
Midnights now I pass wide awake.
I know what it feels to burn in a lazy afternoon.

Yet when agony visits my territory,
Touches the fragile chapter of my heart.
I quietly swim in the ocean of melancholy-
The ocean sings its solace hymn for me.
I desperately look for a comfort to place my eyes:
Were all the struggles meant to end in vain?
Or the sun still smiles behind the clouds?

Road I Follow

I step out of my little territory,
Sweet sunshine welcomes me.
Distant roads I follow alone,
Wind often cares to blow.
Often the clunch of storm,
Sometimes only silence prevails.
I keep bearing what's not to be borne,
And place my final leap to my home-
Conquering the world alone.

Wishes

May all my mistakes turn into flowers,
May all my grieves become birds.
May all my happiness redouble-
When I share them with someone.

May my mistakes tell me a story,
A fable I will never forget.
Yet the grief must go away,
For pain is not a thing to stay.

May my happiness sing a song,
Lyrics embracing everyone.
Yet happiness must not be my own,
For happiness cannot be enjoyed alone.

Our Race

We don't know the road we follow,
We don't know why we do.
We don't combat no battle no more,
We only fight against our soul.

We don't ornate a truth these days,
We cannot part with lies' maze.
Still we don't go against the truth.
We just color lies- follow the truth's race.

Prudent we are, we don't estimate a future.
Perceiving the wreck, we don't fight no longer.
Except for us, we seek for a success so rare:
We only rush till our end.

We don't know where we are going,
We don't know why.

Decide

The boy at his knee,
Handed red roses sparkling

Oh, lady beauty-
Would you care for the love?
Feel elated and offer some?

Or-
Would you start reasoning?
You should solely follow your dreams-
Giving no chance for the heart to bleed?

Or-
You would evade it all?
Leaving him alone-
Unanswered.

Oh, Lady beauty-
The boy still at his knee
Red roses still sparkling
Here is the place
And now is the time-
Take the decision, hereby.

You

And I'd fill my math script
Writing all about you.
About all the short talks,
All the laughter and the stalks,
Together we did, too.

I wanted to tell you how it is,
To look back in time, but this-
I afraid wasn't meant to last.

And I beg you, please-
I had long nights before you came,
And my life's now a mess.
I need someone to hold on to-
And it's always you.

Then I dreamt last night,
That you are completely gone.
I wonder if it comes true,
For I can't have you forever.
For you might get someone better,
For my love might get scattered.
I hate the dream I had last night,
But I'll never hate you.

Love At Its Nineties

A day long poem,
A love that's a shame,
A heart that's void,
A letter ending the game.
There's lot of storm, bicker and mist-
With you and me- protagonist.

I wonder who came closer first,
Who thought about love and lust.

Who versed dreams as the necklace on my neck,
Who fought for the perfect house for a family to make.

Who began the chasm, who began the curb?
Who tried thei' best to salvage this love.

I hardly remember who love had been
For we both have somewhat grown so mean.

I forgot what loving feels to be
Since chaos took a hand on that feelings' custody.

I wonder how time fades time,
With love, commitment accompanied by.

And now as this love is dying fresh,
It's too a part of love that we embrace.

Alone

Why do the stars flicker alone?
Why does the sun have never had a mate?
So does the moon never had a friend.

Why every great creations around
Have the solitary trait to show.
And why do they accompany humans,
With themselves being alone?

Why don't they feel never sad,
Why would they fake a elated smile?
Do they even try to look happy?
Or it's we who assume that they be?

After You Left

With your smile that I felt as pearls,
Pearls that sparkle every in a while.
With your eyes with the depth,
The depth that looks into everything implicit.
With your rhetoric phrases that you utter,
You snatched my heart from me.
Now my soul is a pensive butterfly,
Weave delicate yet sullen feat.

I often sob with the sound of a smile-
With the placidity of abstinence.
I prorogue the gusty surge of my heart-
For something yet to compliance.

And since no light, no chandeliers lit me up,
No stars tried to lift my heart.
I won't call for your love no more.
Probably I'll crouch back the heart of my own.

Her

Such a woman she was
Who sacrificed her life.
What a beauty she held,
For she endured this cage.

I remember her from elementary grades,
She had ocean depth of eyes,
She would look with penetrating sight.
I would see her growing in front of my eyes,
How she's gone through the stings of her life.
I know the scars of her heart-
She had been a living star.
I have thousands times dived deep into her wit,
I do believe God sent her as a gift.

All she did, she never did for her,
Immolating her dreams, all her spurs.

She had sacrificed her life,
She had endured this cage.
Such a woman she had been-
What a beauty she had held.

Two Directions

Two directions divided the road,
Both is to prosperity.
You lose one if you chose another,
You lose both if you don't walk.

Two directions divided the road,
Both have a chance of destruction.
Both ask you to hold your breath,
And walk among the stings awake.

Both directions have fulfillment,
Both have a chance to thrive.
Both take a hell of a pain,
Both takes love for something to gain.

Two directions both resemble your desire.
Not both are equally walked,
Yet both are equally hard-
Which one would you walk?

Beauty

November rain keeps coming each year,
It drenches the sunny days.
Water on the road glitters all day long.
November rain never fails to come back.

And a passive wind blows the city down.

I fail to decide the beauty of it.
I tend to forget the criteria of beauty.
So I decide not to think of it.
No ugly has the ugliness
That an ugly heart bears.
No beauty has the beauty
If no heart bears.

Sadness, My River

A sadness, I call it a river-
A river with water-
Kingfishers around, fishes abandoned.
A river with its depth you cannot figure
out from the outside.
A sadness, is like a river,
Where the flow ends you cannot measure.
You only swim through it,
Not knowing where it ends.
A sadness is truly a river-
It soaks you to your end,
If you cannot swim till the edge.

A river swallows you, like the sadness do.
A river directs you with its flow,
The same power as sadness grabs.
A river, mighty enough-
often to make you give it up.

And a river,
Is beautiful.
A river-
Necessary.
A river feels ecstatic
A river makes nostalgic
A river has an end,
Crowning the shore- worth the pain.
It has the beauty to hold your heart,
Giving the meaning of your life a thought.
A river teaches for things not to hold on to
Exactly the same things that sadness do.

Lover, My Tree

There was a tree in my patio,
That had roots deep into the earth
That tree was a shelter.
I often wonder how many birds,
Countless of insects,
Did the tree offer place.
The tree had been a world for them,
Getting shed, shelter, food and everything else.

The tree had been a shelter for me too-

All along when I'd need someone to hug,
Maybe to cry, holding someone tight,
Probably only a shadow of affection towards me,
It had never been anything else but the tree.
I would sit beneath its tender branches;
I would let it's leaves sing to me.

There most often would be sourcing heat of the sun,
There would be thunders too in the monsoon;
There would be freezing wind when winter would come.
Enduring it all, the tree would stand.

And I could never think of cutting it off,
But as destined to be,
One day,
I had to free the tree;
I had to free the birds,
Asking the insects to find a different shelter.

And thus,
The thing that I loved the most;
Thus the thing I once clung to life;
Thus the thing that offered me love,
I had to push that away.
I had to push my love away.
I had to push my life away.
I had to cut the tree.

And I only let my heart to bleed,
For not holding on to the things I certainly could keep.

My Mother

I wake up in the morning,
Look in the mirror.
The mirror reflects my face,
I look like my mother.

I smile at the reflection,
It smiles back.
The dimples on my chin,
The carves of my lips-
I smile like my mother.

On some hot summer noon,
As I get drenched with sweat,
As I bathe myself wet,
I smell like my mother.

And in the evening as I stop,
Gaze the sky full of stars,
I gaze like my mother.

And when I greet,
Sit and talk with my friends,
I talk like my mother.

Then when I express my thoughts,
Word what my mind has got,
They'd stare at me and decide,
I think like my mother.

For always as I adore the nature,
Its creations with heart,

As I love every spring,
I love like my mother.

Sometimes, there crisis comes-
It distracts life and its forms.
But I survive them with my caliber
And they assure: I do it like my mother.

And when years will pass,
There will be days I wouldn't see her,
I might not recall many traits she own,
But I will always know:
My mother was like me,
I am my mother.

This City

The city from a distant view
Is a silhouette of some gloom.
The city is of dust and rust,
Not a flower happens to bloom.
The city is morose, gray of the cold of sins.
The city knows no waiting hours,
Rush is its desperate soul.
This city with season never changes its fit,
Though it changes so frequently.
This city, no love, might it deserve.
No love could it offer us back.
Yet, this city, truly, owns my heart.

Midnight Town

The sky was dark and dusty,
Dusty was the road as we walk.
Walk beside the river is a whim,
Whim of sky too who reflect thee.

The river water was crystal-
Crystal was the reflection of the moon.
Moon knows she embellishes the town,
Town that has its root to gloom.

The town walks in dead night,
Night awakes its lorn souls.
Souls that are trodden beneath green grasses,
Grasses embrace my feet as I walk,
Walk beside the river is a whim,
Whim of sky too who reflect thee.

I See My Death By The Water Fountain

Brutal-
As it might seem when you face such life.
You might try to escape; maybe you wanna hide.

Slow-
Days look like a fallen sky,
You fail to cover the flaws the hard you try.

Beauties-
They only come and go,
Illustrating maze to and fro.

For I-
Could never care enough,
For the brutalities beauties craft.

For I-
Never understood the hoax of blue,
Could never stop myself craving for you.

And I-
As I know how frail this life is,
I'd strand everything for nature's bliss.

And I-
Will ode a life of earth, wind and rain,
For I see my death by the water fountain.

Spring Came Once

Spring once visited this city.
Flowers awaiting inmates-
New leaves barely sprouted.
Still were the sullen air of winter,
So were the dust in the path I follow me home.
In the dark,
Or exposed to light.
Void filled with fulfillment:
Every scenario embracing winter.

Winter comes and go,
Winter comes and go.
Thus regulates the seasons though.

This city could never dream of spring,
Yet spring had once come.
Only once:
No ingression note, nothing splendor,
No wreath or frivolity;
Devoid all came silently the spring.
Silent yet royal was its leap.
The only time spring visited the city.
What was that pain,
What was that peace,
What was that grief, what that was gained.
The spring merely came,
And went away.
Spring never visited the city no more,
Let spring never visit the city no more.
This city don't know how to guest a spring,
Let them not come those who are meant to leave,
Let them not blend illusion who are meant not to last.

Let only winter prevail,

That winter paints our wails,
That winter warms the heart.
The winter so morose.
The winter alives no hope.
No love does the winter offer.
Yet offers the spur to embrace the soul.

If not meant to last flowers of this spring.
If not to withstand rain, storm or pain,
Let the winter conquer its flame.

Author

Oh author!
Put me in your poem.
Write me down inch by inch,
Tell your readers, I'm a girl: not so fair.
Describe my beauty just how it is.

Oh author,
I have a tan skin,
With wrinkles on my cheeks.
I don't have ocean blue eyes,
Shame! Mine's worth hardly admire.
I have a jawline some middle-aged women get,
I have scars that I couldn't erase.

Author, I know,
You might want to portrait me beautiful,
A bit smarter, much a bit happier too.
I know you worship beauty,
I know you'd do it here too.
How about I beg you not to?

Author, I beg,
I know my beauty is a shame,
Still I beg you to pen
Pen me however I am.
Let your readers know,
Only beauty is not what gets admired.
Frame them the scars I hide behind my eyes,
Tell them the tale of my elation getting surmised.
Utter the venoms I face per day,
For not owning beauty, unlike them.

Author, I know-
You will ode my plainness with some word so kind.
You might find me a place in your verse.
But this world, Author, is nicely rough.
Please don't hide my tears in your words,
Let your readers know the blue of my heart.
Tell your readers the brutal of the earth.

Don't be a poet, a worshiper of humanity.
For once, author, reflect the society.

The Last Rain

This will be the last poem I will write.
Less of a poem but a story I will pen-
Story of a pensive girl and her cherished rain.

It was winter,
Not an unusual time for rain to come.
Yet the girl wholeheartedly wished for some.
She had an ardent desire to dance in rain-
With muds underneath her feet,
Flowers over leaves,
Birds on branches-
She wanted rain to sound like teardrops,
She wished for birds to chirp in the backgr'nd.
Maybe fairies from heaven would come to earth-
And write down each melody getting birth.

But she didn't get any of it-
She had no escape from the prison she lived.
Neither did the rain showed its face,
For seasons have their internal race.

The girl falling trapped, one day died-
Without dances in the rain with flies.
My poems failed to offer her needed warmth
So I decided my pen to stop.

THE END

www.ingramcontent.com/pod-product-compliance
Lightning Source LLC
LaVergne TN
LVHW041251150826
845673LV00008B/2546
9798368020297